MAX LUCADO

JUST IN CASE
You Ever
Wonder

Illustrated by Toni Goffe

Tommy NELSON®

A Division of Thomas Nelson Publishers

NASHVILLE DALLAS MEXICO CITY RIO DE JANEIRO

JUST IN CASE YOU EVER WONDER
Text © 1992, 2011 by Max Lucado
Illustrations © 1992, 2011 by Toni Goffe
Karen Hill, Executive Editor for Max Lucado

Published in Nashville, Tennessee, by Tommy Nelson. Tommy Nelson is a registered trademark of Thomas Nelson, Inc.

Thomas Nelson, Inc. titles may be purchased in bulk for educational, business, fund-raising, or sales promotional use. For information, please e-mail SpecialMarkets@ThomasNelson.com.

ISBN 978-1-4003-1958-9

The Library of Congress has cataloged the earlier edition as follows:
Lucado, Max.
    Just in case you ever wonder / by Max Lucado; illustrated by Toni Goffe
        p. cm.
Summary: A parent tells a child how special she is, both to the parent and to God.
    ISBN 978-1-4003-0878-1 (2006 edition)
    ISBN 978-0-8499-0978-8 (1992 edition)
    [1. Parent and child—Fiction. 2. Christian life—Fiction.]
    I. Goffe, Toni, ill. II. Title.
    PZ7.L9684Ju 1992
    [E]—dc20

92-25059
CIP
AC

Printed in Malaysia

13 14 15 TWP 5 4 3

Mfr.: Tien Wah Press Ltd. / Malaysia / October 2013 / PPO# 9272790

Jenna, Andrea, and Sara, this book
is for you—just in case you ever wonder.

Long, long ago God made a decision—
a very important decision . . .
one that I'm really glad He made.
He made the decision to make you.

The same hands that made the stars *made you*.

The same hands that made the canyons *made you*.

The same hands that made the trees and the

moon and the sun *made you*.

That's why you are so special. God made you.

He made you in a very special way.

He made your eyes so they would twinkle.

He made your mouth so you could smile.

He made your laugh so you could giggle.

God made you like no one else.

If you looked all over the world—in every city in every
house—there would be no one else like you . . .

   no one with your eyes,

   no one with your mouth,

   no one with your laugh.

You are very, very special.

And since you are so special, God wanted to put you in just the right home . . .

where you would be warm when it's cold,

where you'd be safe when you're afraid,

where you'd have fun and learn about heaven.

So, after lots of looking for just the right family, God sent you to me. And I'm so glad He did.

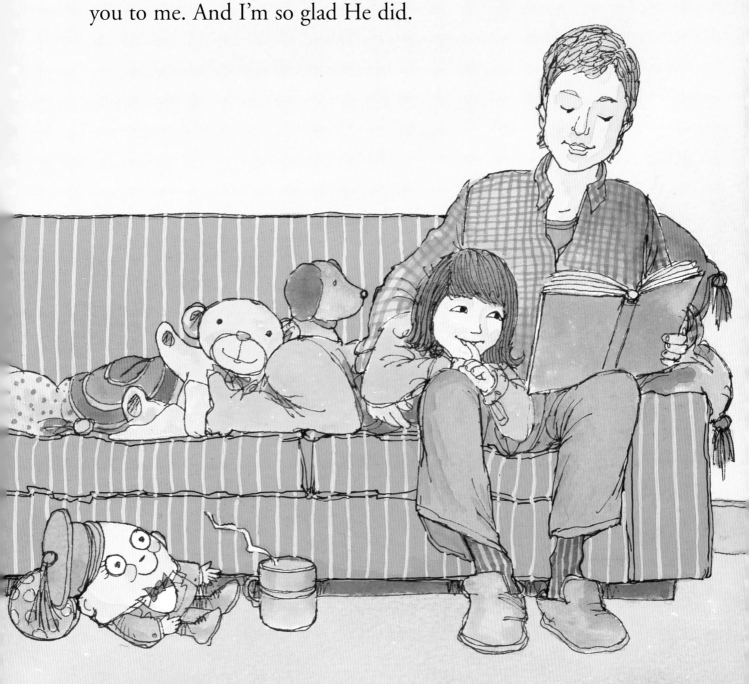

I'll never forget the first time I saw you . . .

your eyes were closed,

your fingers were curled in two little fists,

your cheeks were puffy and round.

I knew in my heart God had sent someone very wonderful

for me to take care of.

Your first night with me I heard every sound you made:

I heard you gurgle,

I heard you sniff,

I heard your little lips smack.

I heard you cry when you wanted to eat, and I fed you.

You're bigger now and do more things.

You can walk and run.

You can play and talk.

You can eat and sing and look at books.

You're not a little baby anymore.

But as you grow and change, some things will
stay the same.

    I'll always love you.

    I'll always hug you.

    I'll always be on your side.

And I want you to know that . . . just in case
you ever wonder.

Remember I'm here for you.
On dark nights when you hear noises in your closet,
call me.

When you see monsters in the shadows, call me.

On hard days when kids are mean and don't treat you like they should, come to me.

If your grades are bad and your teacher is mad, come to me . . . 'cause I love you.

And I always will, just in case you ever wonder.

Most of all, I'll be here to teach you about God.

He loves you.

He protects you.

He and His angels are always watching over you.

And God wants me to make sure you know about heaven.

It's a wonderful place.

There are no tears there.

No monsters.

No mean people.

You never have to say "good-bye,"
   or "good night,"
   or "I'm hungry."
You never get cold or sick or afraid.

In heaven you are so close to God that He will hug you, just like I hug you. It's going to be wonderful. I will be there, too. I promise. We will be there together, forever. Remember that . . .

just in case you ever wonder.